"WHAT BEINGS
BENEATH A SUN
ARE JEWELS OF
GAS AND SILVER
STARS OF ICE?"

STANISLAW LEM
Born 1921, Lwów, Poland
Died 2006, Kraków, Poland

Stories taken from *Mortal Engines*, first published in the
United States of America by The Seabury Press, 1977
and first published in Penguin Classics, 2016.

LEM IN PENGUIN MODERN CLASSICS
The Cyberiad
Fiasco (forthcoming)
The Futurological Congress
Mortal Engines
The Star Diaries

STANISLAW LEM

The Three Electroknights

Translated by Michael Kandel

PENGUIN BOOKS

PENGUIN CLASSICS

UK | USA | Canada | Ireland | Australia
India | New Zealand | South Africa

Penguin Books is part of the Penguin Random House group
of companies whose addresses can be found at
global.penguinrandomhouse.com.

This selection first published 2018

001

English translation copyright © The Continuum
Publishing Company, 1977

Set in 11.2/13.75 pt Dante MT Std
Typeset by Jouve (UK), Milton Keynes
Printed in Great Britain by Clays Ltd, St Ives plc

ISBN: 978-0-241-33939-8

www.greenpenguin.co.uk

MIX
Paper from
responsible sources
FSC® C018179

Penguin Random House is committed to a
sustainable future for our business, our readers
and our planet. This book is made from Forest
Stewardship Council® certified paper.

Contents

The Three Electroknights

Once there lived a certain great inventor-constructor who, never flagging, thought up unusual devices and fashioned the most amazing mechanisms. He built himself a digital midget-widget that sweetly sang, and he named it a 'bird'. A bold heart served as his symbol, and every atom that passed through his hands bore that mark, so that afterwards scientists did marvel to find in among the atomic spectra flickering valentines. He made many useful machines, both large and small, until the whimsical notion came to him to unite life and death in one and thereby accomplish the impossible. He decided to construct intelligent beings out of water, oh but not in that monstrous way which probably first occurred to you. No, the thought of bodies soft and wet was foreign to him, he abhorred it as do we all. His intention was to construct from water beings truly beautiful and wise, therefore crystalline. He selected a planet far removed from any sun, cut mountains of ice from its frozen ocean and out of those carved the Cryonids. They bore this name, for only in the intense cold could they exist, and in the sunless void. Before very long they had built themselves cities and palaces of ice, and, as any heat whatever threatened them with extinction, they trapped polar lights in large transparent vessels and with these illumined their dwellings. He who among them was more important, the more polar lights he had, lemon yellow and silver. And they all lived happily, and, loving not only light but precious stones, they grew famous for their gems. The gems, cut and ground from frozen gases, added color to their eternal night, in which burned – like imprisoned spirits – the thin polar lights, resembling enchanted nebulae in blocks of crystal. More than one cosmic conqueror wished to possess these riches, for all Cryonia was visible at the greatest distance, its facets twinkling like a jewel rotated slowly on black velvet. And so adventurers came to Cryonia, to try their hand in battle. The first to arrive was the electroknight Brass, whose step was as a big bell tolling, but no sooner had he set foot upon the sheets of ice than they melted from the heat, and down he plunged into the icy deep, and the waters closed over him. Like an insect in amber he remains, to this very day, encased in a mountain of ice at the bottom of the Cryonian sea.

The fate of Brass did not deter other daredevils. After him came the electroknight Iron, who had drunk liquid helium until his steel innards gurgled and the frost that formed upon his armor gave him the appearance of a snow giant. But in swooping to the surface of the planet he heated up from the atmospheric friction, the liquid helium evaporated out of him with a whistle, and he himself, glowing red, landed on some crags of ice, which opened instantly. He pulled himself out, belching steam, similar to a boiling geyser, but everything he touched became a white cloud from which snow fell. So he sat and waited for himself to cool, and when the little stars of snow no longer melted on his shoulder plates, he sought to rise and go out into battle, but the oil had congealed in his joints and he could not even straighten his back. He sits there still, and the falling snow has made of him a white mountain, from which only the tip of his helmet protrudes. They call it Iron Mountain, and in its eye sockets gleams a frozen stare.

News of the fate of his predecessors reached the third electroknight, Quartz, who in the day appeared as a polished lens, and at night as a mirror filled with stars. He did not fear that the oil in his limbs would congeal, for he hadn't any, nor that the ice floes would crack beneath his feet, for he could become as cold as he liked. There was one thing only he had to avoid and this was prolonged thought, for it made his quartz brain grow warm and that could destroy him. But he resolved to protect himself and gain victory over the Cryonids by the simple expedient of not thinking. He flew to the planet, and was so chilled by his long voyage through the eternal galactic night, that the iron meteors that grazed his breast in flight shattered into shivers with a tinkling sound. He set down on the white snows of Cryonia, beneath its black sky like a jug of stars, and, resembling a transparent glass, began to ponder his next move, but the snow around him was already darkening and starting to steam.

'Uh-oh', Quartz said to himself, 'not good! That's all right, just don't think, and it's in the bag!'

He resolved to repeat this single phrase no matter what happened, for it required no mental effort and therefore would not heat him up at all. So Quartz proceeded through the snowy wild thoughtlessly and at random, in order to preserve his coolness. He walked thus, till finally he came to the ice walls of the capital of the Cryonids, Frigida. He charged and struck the battlements with his head, until the sparks flew, but that accomplished nothing.

'Let's try it differently!' he said to himself and considered how much two times two would be. Reflecting upon this, his head became a trifle warmer, so he rammed the glittering walls a second time, but made only a small dent.

'Not enough!' he said to himself. 'Let's try something harder. How much is three times five?'

Now his head was surrounded by a sizzling cloud, for in contact with such intense mentation the snow instantly boiled, so Quartz stepped back, gathered up speed, struck and went straight through the wall, and through two palaces behind it, plus three houses of the lesser Counts of Hoar, fell upon a great staircase, clutched the stalactite banister, but the steps were like a skating rink. He jumped up quickly, for now everything about him was melting and in this way he could go tumbling down through the entire city, down into the ice abyss, where he would be forever frozen.

'That's all right! Just don't think! It's in the bag!' he told himself, and sure enough, he cooled off at once.

So he went out of the tunnel of ice which he had melted, and found himself in a great square lit up on every side by polar lights that winked in emerald and silver on their crystal pillars.

Then towards him issued forth, sparkling and starry, an enormous knight, the commander of the Cryonids, Boreal. Quartz pulled himself together and leaped to the attack, and the other closed with him, and there was a crash, as when two icebergs in the middle of the Northern Sea collide. The gleaming right arm of Boreal fell away, sheared off at the socket, but, nothing daunted, he

5

turned, so that his chest, broad as a glacier (which in point of fact it was), faced the enemy. The enemy meanwhile gathered up momentum and once again rammed him savagely. And, since quartz is harder and more dense than ice, Boreal split with a roar like an avalanche moving down a rocky slope, and he lay, all shattered in the glow of the polar lights, that witnessed his defeat.

'In the bag! Just keep it up!' said Quartz, and tore from the fallen warrior jewels of wondrous beauty: rings set with hydrogen, clasps and medallions that shone like diamonds, though cut from the trio of noble gases – argon, krypton and xenon. When however he admired them, the warmth of that emotion warmed him, consequently the diamonds and sapphires evaporated with a hiss beneath his touch, so that he held nothing – save a few droplets of dew, which also quickly vanished.

'Uh-oh! Can't admire either! No matter! Just don't think!' he said to himself and forged on into the heart of the conquered city. In the distance he saw a mighty figure approaching. This was Albucid the White, General-Mineral, whose massive breast was crisscrossed with rows of icicle medals and the Great Star of Rime upon a glacial ribbon; that keeper of the royal treasures barred the way to Quartz, who bore down on him like a storm and smote him in a thunderclap of ice. Then Prince Astrobert, Lord of the Black Hail, came to the aid of

Albucid; this time the electroknight had met his match, for the Prince had on his costly nitrogen armor, tempered in helium. So fierce was the cold that he gave off, it robbed Quartz of his impetus, weakened his movements, and even the polar lights grew pale, such was the breath of Absolute Zero that spread about. Quartz pulled up and thought: 'Yipes! What's going on?' – and from that great astonishment his brain heated, the Absolute Zero grew summery, and before his eyes Astrobert himself began to break up into chunks, with thunder accompanying the death throes, till only a heap of black ice, dripping drops like tears, remained in a puddle on the battlefield.

'In the bag!' said Quartz to himself. 'Just don't think, but if you have to think, then think! Either way you win!' And he pressed on, and his steps rang, as though someone were hammering at crystals; and as he pounded through the streets of Frigida, its inhabitants peered out at him from under the white eaves, despair in their hearts. He was hurtling along like a mad meteor across the Milky Way, when in the distance he noticed a small and solitary figure. This was none other than Baryon, known as the Brrr, the greatest sage among the Cryonids. Quartz built up speed, intending to crush him in a single blow, but the other stepped out of the way and raised two fingers; Quartz had no idea what this might mean, but he turned and went full tilt at his opponent, yet once again at the last moment Baryon stepped aside and quickly raised one finger. Quartz was somewhat surprised at this and slowed his pace, though he had already turned around and was about to charge. He wondered, and water began to pour from the neighboring homes, but he did not see this, for now Baryon was showing him a circle with his fingers and swiftly moving the thumb of the other hand back and forth through it. Quartz thought and thought of what those silent gestures were supposed to represent, while a chasm opened up beneath his feet, black water gushed forth, and he sank like a stone, and before he had time to say, 'That's all right, just don't think!' – he was no more among the living. Later the Cryonids, grateful to Baryon for their deliverance, asked him what it was he had intended to convey through the signs he made to the terrible rogue electroknight.

'It's quite simple, really', replied the sage. 'Two fingers meant that there were two of us, he and I together. One finger, that soon only I would be left. Then I showed him the circle, indicating that the ice was opening around him and the ocean's black abyss would swallow him forever. He failed to understand the first, and likewise the second and the third.'

'O great wise one!' exclaimed the astonished Cryonids. 'How could you have given such signs to the dread invader?! Think what would have happened had he comprehended and disdained surprise! Surely then his mind would not have heated, nor would he have plunged into the bottomless abyss . . .'

'Pooh, I had no fear of that', said Baryon the Brrr with an icy smile. 'I knew all along he would not understand. If he'd had a grain of sense to begin with, he never would have come here. For what use to a being that lives beneath a sun are jewels of gas and silver stars of ice?'

And they in turn marveled at the wisdom of the sage and so departed, satisfied, each to the comforting chill of his own hearth. After this no one ever again attempted to invade Cryonia, the entire Universe not having any more such fools, though some say there are plenty still, they merely do not know the way.

The White Death

Aragena was a planet built up on the inside, because its ruler, Metameric – who in the equatorial plane extended three hundred and sixty degrees and thereby encircled his kingdom, being not only its lord but also its shield – wishing to protect his devoted subjects, the Enterites, against cosmic invasion, forbade the moving of anything whatever, even of the smallest pebble, upon the surface of the globe. Therefore the continents of Aragena lay wild and barren, and only the ax-blows of lightning hewed its flint mountain ridges, while meteors carved the land with craters. But ten miles beneath the surface unfolded a region of exuberant industry; the Enterites, hollowing out their mother planet, filled its interior with crystal gardens and cities of silver and gold; they raised up, inside-out, houses in the shape of dodecahedrons and icosahedrons, and also hyperboloid palaces, in whose shining cupolas you could see yourself magnified twenty thousand times, as in a hall of giants – for the Enterites were fond of splendor and geometry, and were topnotch builders besides. With a system of pipes they pumped light into the heart of the planet, filtering it now through emeralds, now diamonds, and now rubies, and thanks to this they had their choice of dawn, or noon, or rosy dusk; and so enamored were they of their own forms, that their whole world served them as a mirror. They had vehicles of crystal, set in motion by the breath of heated gases, windowless, since entirely transparent, and while they traveled they beheld themselves reflected in the walls of palaces and temples as marvelously multiple projections, gliding, touching, iridescent. They even had their own sky, where in webs of molybdenum and vanadium flashed spinels and rock crystal, which they cultivated in fire.

The hereditary and at the same time perpetual ruler was Metameric, for he possessed a cold, beautiful and many-membered frame, and in the first of his members resided the mind; when that grew old, after thousands of years, when the crystal networks had been worn away from much administrative thinking, its authority was taken over by the next member, and thus it went, for of these he had ten billion. Metameric himself descended from the Aurigens, whom he had never seen, and all he knew of them was that when they were faced with doom at the hands of certain dreadful beings – beings that engaged in cosmonautics, and for it had abandoned their native suns – the Aurigens locked all their knowledge and hunger for existence into microscopic atom seeds, and with them fertilized the rocky soil of Aragena. They gave it that name, a name like their own, but never set armored foot upon its rocks, so as not to put their cruel pursuers on the scent; they perished, every last one, having this consolation only, that their enemies – called the pale race – did not even suspect that the Aurigens had not been totally wiped out. The Enterites, who sprang from Metameric, did not share his knowledge of their own uncommon origin: the history of the terrible demise of the Aurigens, as well as that of the rise of the Enterites, was recorded in a black vesuvian protocrystal hidden at the very core of the planet. So much the better was this history known and remembered by their ruler.

Out of the stony and magnetic ground that the resourceful builders cut away in expanding their subterranean kingdom, Metameric ordered made a row of reefs, which were cast into space. These orbited the planet in infernal circles, closing off all access to it. Cosmic mariners therefore avoided that region, known as the Black Rattler, for there enormous chunks of flying basalt and porphyry collided continually, giving rise to whole swarms of meteors, and the place was the breeding ground for all the comet heads, all the bolides and rock asteroids that today clutter the entire system of the Scorpion.

The meteors also pounded in waves of stone the ground of Aragena, bombarded it, furrowed and plowed it; with fountains of fire-spouting impacts they turned night into day, and day – with thick clouds of dust – into night. But not the least vibration reached the realm of the Enterites. Anyone who dared approach their planet would have seen, if first he did not dash his ship against the vortices of stone, a craggy globe, rather like a skull all crater-eaten. Even the gate that led to the underground levels was given by the Enterites the appearance of a sundered stone.

For thousands of years no one visited the planet, still Metameric did not relax his injunction of strict vigilance for an instant.

It happened however that one day a group of Enterites, who went up on the surface, came across what seemed to be a giant goblet, its stem embedded in a pile of boulders and its concave cup, which faced the sky, crushed and punctured in a dozen places. Immediately the polysage-astromariners were sent for, and they announced that what they had before them was the wreck of some foreign starcraft from unknown parts. The vessel was quite large. Only up close could one see that it had the shape of a slender cylinder, nose buried in the rock, that it was covered by a thick layer of soot and cinder; the construction of the rear, goblet-like section brought to mind the sweeping vaults of their vast subterranean palaces. Up from the depths crawled pincered machines, which with extreme care lifted the mysterious ship from where it lay and carried it back down to the interior. Afterwards a group of Enterites smoothed over the hole created by the nose of the vessel, in order that there be no trace of foreign presence on the planet's surface, and the basalt gate was closed with a hollow boom.

In the main research laboratory, sumptuous and full of luster, rested the black hulk, looking much like some charred log, but the scientists, familiar with this sort of thing, trained upon it the polished surfaces of their most radiant crystals, and with diamond bits they opened the first outer shell. Beneath it was another, of amazing whiteness, which disconcerted them somewhat, and when that shell too was pierced by carborundum drills, there appeared a third, impenetrable, and – set in it hermetically – a door, but they were unable to open it.

The eldest scientist, Afinor, carefully examined the closing mechanism on that door; it turned out that for the lock to be released, one had to activate it with a spoken word. They did not know the word, they had no way of knowing it. For a long time they tried different ones, like 'Universe', 'Stars', 'Eternal Flight', but the door never moved.

'Methinks we do wrong, attempting to open the vessel without the knowledge of King Metameric', said Afinor at last. 'As a child I heard a legend telling of white creatures who throughout the Universe hunt down all life born of metal, and annihilate it for the sake of vengeance, which . . .'

Here he broke off and with the others stared in horror at the side of the ship, large as a wall, for at his last words the door, till now inert, suddenly stirred and rolled aside. The word that had opened it was 'Vengeance'.

The scientists cried for military assistance and, soon having it at hand, when the sparkthrowers were held in readiness, entered the still and stuffy darkness of the ship, lighting their way with crystals blue and white.

The machinery was to a great extent shattered. For hours they wandered among its ruins, seeking a crew, but no crew did they find, nor any sign of one. They considered whether the ship itself might not be a thinking being, for such oftentimes were very large: in size their king exceeded the unknown vessel many thousandfold, yet *he* was an entity. However the junctures of electrical thought which they uncovered were all quite small and loosely connected; the foreign ship therefore could be nothing but a flying machine, and without a crew would be as dead as stone.

In one of the corners of the deck, against the very

armorplated wall, the scientists came upon a puddle, a ruddy sort of spatter that colored their silver fingers when they drew near; from this puddle they extricated shreds of an unknown garment, wet and red, and in addition a few silvers of something not very hard, fairly chalky. They knew not why, but a feeling of dread came over them as they stood there in the dark, in the prickling light of their crystals. But now the king had learned of this event; his messengers arrived at once, with the strictest orders to destroy the foreign vessel including everything that was upon it, and in particular the king commanded that the foreign travelers be committed to atomic fire.

The scientists replied that there was no one at all on board, only darkness and broken fragments, metal entrails and some dust speckled with tiny stains of red. The royal messenger started and immediately ordered the atomic piles to be ignited.

'In the name of the King!' he said. 'The red that you have found is the harbinger of doom! It carries the white death, which knows nothing but to wreak vengeance upon those whose only crime is their existence . . .'

'If that was the white death, it can threaten us no longer, for the vessel is without life and whoever sailed it has perished in the ring of fortified reefs,' they answered.

'Infinite is the power of those pallid beings, that if they die, they are reborn anew countless times, far from the mighty suns! Carry out your orders, O atomizers!'

The wise ones and the scientists were greatly troubled when they heard these words. Still, they did not believe the prophecy of doom, for its likelihood seemed to them remote. Nevertheless they lifted the entire ship from its resting place, smashed it on anvils of platinum and, when it fell apart, immersed the pieces in heavy radiation, so that it was reduced to a myriad of flying atoms, which keep eternal silence, for atoms have no history, all are equal to each other, whether they come from the strongest of stars or from dead planets, or intelligent beings, both good and evil, because matter is the same throughout the Universe and no one need have fear of it.

However they took even these atoms and froze them down into a single lump, and shot that lump out towards the stars, and only then did they say to themselves with relief: 'We are saved. Nothing can happen now.'

But while the platinum hammers had been striking the ship and as it crumbled, from a scrap of cloth besmeared with blood, from a torn-out seam there dropped an invisible spore, a spore so small that even a hundred like it could have been covered by a single grain of sand. And from this spore there hatched – at night, in the dust and ashes among the stones of the cavern – a white bud.

From it sprang a second, a third, a hundredth, and in a gust of air they gave off oxygen and moisture, wherewith rust attacked the flagstones of the mirror cities, and imperceptible threads wound and wove about, incubating in the cool bowels of the Enterites, so that by the time they rose, they carried with them their own deaths. And a year did not pass, and they were stricken down. In the caves machines stood still, the crystal fires went out, a brownish leprosy ate at the sparkling domes, and when the last atomic heat had leaked away, darkness fell, and in that darkness there grew, penetrating the brittle skeletons, invading the rusted skulls, filling the extinguished sockets – a downy, damp, white mold.

King Globares and the Sages

Globares, ruler of Eparida, once summoned his greatest sages to appear before him, and he said:

'Truly, hard is the lot of a king who has learned everything there is to learn, so that what is said to him sounds hollow as a broken jug! I wish to be astounded, yet am bored, I seek stimulation, yet hear wearisome twaddle, I long for novelty, and they treat me to insipid flatteries. Know, O'wise ones, that today I have ordered all my fools and jesters executed, along with my advisers high and low, and this same fate awaits you if you fail to do my bidding. Let each of you tell me the strangest tale he knows, but if it moves me neither to laughter nor to tears, confounds not nor dismays, provides no entertainment nor food for thought – he parts with his head!' The King made a sign and the sages heard the iron step of the myrmidons that surrounded them at the foot of the throne, and whose naked swords did gleam like flame. They were afraid and nudged one another, for none of them wished to risk the King's anger and lay his head upon the block. Finally the first spoke:

'O King and ruler! The strangest tale in all the visible and invisible Universe is without question that of the stellar tribe known in the chronicles as the Awks. From the dawn of their history the Awks did everything opposite compared to all other beings of intelligence. Their ancestors settled on Urdruria, a planet famous for its volcanoes; each year it gives birth to new mountain chains, during which time terrible spasms convulse it, so that nothing remains standing. And, to make the misery of the inhabitants complete, the heavens saw fit to have their globe pass through the Meteor Stream; this for two hundred days out of the year pounds the planet with droves of stone battering rams. The Awks (who at that time were not yet called thus) raised edifices of tempered iron and steel, and themselves they covered with such quantities of steel plates, they resembled walking mounds of armor. Nevertheless the ground opened up during the quakes and swallowed their steel cities, and meteor hammers crushed their suits of armor. When the entire race became threatened with annihilation, its sages gathered and held council, and the first one said: – Our people will not survive in their present form and there is no escape save through transmutation. The earth opens from below in crevices, therefore in order not to fall in, each Awk must possess a base that is wide and flat; the meteors on the other hand come from above, and so each Awk must be sharp-ended at the top. As cones, we will be safe from harm.

'And the second one said: – That is not the way to do it. If the earth opens its jaws wide, it will swallow up a cone as well, and a meteor falling at an angle will pierce its side. The ideal shape is a sphere. For when the ground begins to tremble and heave, a sphere will always roll aside by itself, and a falling meteor will hit its oblique surface and skim off; we should therefore transform ourselves in order to roll onward towards a brighter future.

'And the third one said: – A sphere is subject to being crushed or swallowed up no less than any other material form. No shield exists, which a powerful enough sword cannot penetrate, nor a sword which will not be notched by a hard shield. Matter, O my brothers, means perpetual change, flux and transformation, it is impermanent. Not in *it* should beings truly blessed with intelligence take up residence, but in that which is immutable, eternal and all-perfect, though of this world!

'– And what is that? – inquired the other sages.

'– I shall not tell you, but instead show you! – replied the third. And before their eyes he began to undress; he removed his outer robe, studded with crystals, and the second, gold-embroidered, and the silver trousers, then removed the top of his skull and his breast, then stripped himself with increasing speed and precision, going from joints to couplings, from couplings to bolts, from bolts to filaments, scintillas, till finally he got down to atoms. And then that sage began to shell his atoms, and shelled them so swiftly, nothing could be seen except for his dwindling and his disappearing, yet he proceeded so adroitly and in such great haste, that in the course of those dismantling movements – before the eyes of his flabbergasted fellow sages – he remained as a perfect absence, which was so exact as to be, in a manner of speaking, negatively present. For there where he had had, previously, a single atom, now he did not have that single atom, where a moment ago six had been, six were now missing, in the place where a little screw had been, the lack of a little screw appeared, perfectly faithful and in no wise departing from it. And in this way he became a vacuum, arranged just as was arranged, previously, that which it replaced, namely himself; and no existence interfered with his nonexisting, for he had worked quickly and maneuvered nimbly in order that no particle, no material intrusion should pollute the perfection of the presence of his absence! And the others saw him as a void shaped exactly as he had been only an instant before, they recognized his eyes by the absence of their black color, his face by the missing skyblue shine, and his limbs by the vanished fingers, joints and shoulder-plates! – In this very way, O my brothers – said the One There Not There – through active self-incorporation into nothingness, we shall acquire not only tremendous immunity, but immortality as well. For only matter changes, and nothingness does not accompany it on that path of continual uncertainty, therefore perfection lies in nonbeing, not in being, and we must choose the first, and spurn the latter!

'And they decided, and did accordingly. From then on the Awks were, and are to this day, an invincible race. They owe their existence not to that which is within them, for within them there is nothing, but wholly to that which surrounds them. And when one of them enters a home, he is visible as that home's non-presence, and if he steps into a mist – as its local discontinuity. Thus, in ridding themselves of the vicissitudes of precarious matter, have they made possible the impossible . . .'

'But how then do they travel through the cosmic void, my sage?' asked Globares.

'This alone they cannot do, O King, since the outer void would merge with their own and they would cease to exist as nonexistences concentrated locally. Therefore also they must maintain a constant watch over the

purity of their absence, over the emptiness of their iden-
tities, and this vigilance occupies their time . . . They call
themselves Be-nothings or Nullians . . .'

'Sage', said the King, 'it is a foolish tale you tell, for
how can material diversity be replaced by the uniformity
of that which is not there? Is a rock the same as a house?
Yet surely the lack of a rock may take the same form as
the lack of a house, consequently the one and the other
become as if identical.'

'Sire', the sage defended himself, 'there are different
kinds of nothingness . . .'

'We shall see', said the King, 'what happens when I
order you beheaded. How think you, will the absence of
a head become its presence?' Here the monarch gave a
hideous laugh and motioned to his myrmidons.

'Sire!' cried the sage, already in the grip of their steel
hands. 'You were pleased to laugh, my tale therefore
awoke your mirth, thus in keeping with your given word
you should spare my life!'

'No, I provided my own amusement', said the King.
'Unless, that is, you go along with the joke: if you agree
voluntarily to be beheaded, that will amuse me, and then
'twill be as you wish.'

'I agree!' shouted the sage.

'In that case behead him, seeing that he himself
requests it!' said the King.

'But Sire, I agreed in order that you not behead me . . .'

'If you agree, you must be beheaded,' explained the King. 'And if you do not agree, you will have failed to amuse me, and so then too you must be beheaded . . .'

'No, no, it is the other way around!' the sage cried. 'If I agree, then you, amused, should spare my life, and if I do not agree . . .'

'Enough!' said the King. 'Executioner, do your duty!'

The sword flashed and the sage's head came tumbling down.

After a moment of deathly silence the second of the sages spoke:

'O King and ruler! The strangest of all the stellar tribes is without question the race of the Polyonts, or Multiploids, also called the Pluralites. Each of them has, it is true, only one body, but despite this many legs, and the higher the office held, the greater the number. As far as heads are concerned, they have them as the need arises: each office, among them, carries with it an appropriate head, impoverished families possess in common only one, the wealthy on the other hand accumulate in their safes a variety, for different occasions: they have, then, morning heads and evening, strategic heads in case of war and high-speed heads when they are in a hurry, as well as cool-and-level heads, explosive heads, heads for passion, dalliance, marriage and funerals, and thus they are equipped for every situation in life.'

'Is that it?' asked the King.

'No, Sire!' replied the sage, who saw it wasn't going well for him. 'The Pluralites also derive their name from the fact that all are linked up with their ruler, and in such a way that if ever the majority deems the royal actions to be harmful to the general welfare, that ruler loses his cohesion and disintegrates . . .'

'Unoriginal, if not – regicidal!' the King said darkly. 'Since you yourself, sage, have had so much to say upon the topic of heads, perhaps you can tell me: Am I now going to order you beheaded, or not?'

– If I say he will – quickly thought the sage – then he will indeed, for he is ill-disposed toward me. If I say he will not, that will catch him unawares, and if he is surprised, he will have to set me free according to his promise. – And he said:

'No, Sire, you will not behead me.'

'You are mistaken', said the King. 'Executioner, do your duty!'

'But Sire!' cried the sage, already seized by the myrmidons, 'did not my words surprise you? Did you not expect me to say, rather, that you would order me beheaded?'

'Your words did not surprise me,' answered the King,

'for they were dictated by fear, which you have written on your face. Enough! Off with his head!'

And with a clang the head of the second sage went rolling across the marble floor. The third and oldest of the sages watched this scene with complete calm. And when the King again demanded an amazing tale, he said:

'O King! I could tell you a story truly extraordinary, but this I shall not do, for I would rather make you honest than cause you to be amazed. Thus will I force you to behead me, not under the paltry pretext of this game into which you seek to turn your killing, but in a manner true to your nature, a nature which, though cruel, dares not work its pleasure without donning first the mask of falsehood. For you wished to behead us, so that it would be said afterwards that the King had put to death fools who pretended to wisdom not theirs. It is my desire, however, that the truth be told, and so will I keep silent.'

'No, I will not give you to the executioner now,' said the King. 'I sincerely and honestly crave something novel. You sought to anger me, but I can curb my anger till the proper time. I say to you: Speak, and you will save perchance not only your own self. The tale you tell may border even on lese majesty, which indeed you have already permitted yourself, but this time it must be an affront so monstrous as to become a compliment, and a compliment of such dimensions as to constitute in turn an outrage! Try then at a single blow both to elevate and humiliate, both to magnify and mortify your King!'

A silence fell. Those present made small motions, as if seeing how firmly their heads still rested on their shoulders.

The third sage seemed plunged in thought. At last he said:

'O King, I shall carry out your wish, and reveal to you the reason why. I shall do this thing for the sake of all those present here, for my own sake, yes and for yours also, in order that it not be said in years to come that there lived a king who by his caprice destroyed wisdom in his kingdom. Even if that *is* the case at this moment, even if your wish has little importance or none at all, my task is to impart value to that passing whim, to turn it into something meaningful and lasting – and therefore I shall speak . . .'

'Old one, enough now of your introduction, which once again borders on lese majesty, and without coming anywhere near a compliment,' said the King angrily. 'Speak!'

'O King, you abuse your power,' replied the sage, 'yet your abuses are nothing compared to those which became the lot of your remote ancestor, unknown to you, who was also the founder of the Eparid dynasty. This great-great-great-grandfather of yours, Allegoric, likewise abused his royal power. To give you some idea of the enormity of what he did, I ask you to look out upon yon night horizon, visible through the upper windows of the palace hall.' The King gazed up at the sky, starry and clear, and the old one continued slowly:

'Behold and hearken! Everything that is, is ridiculed. No station, however high, is proof against ridicule, for there always will be ones who mock even the majesty of a king. Laughter strikes at thrones and realms. Nations make fun of other nations, or of themselves. It even happens that fun is made of what does not exist – have not mythological gods been laughed at? Even things grimly serious and solemn – tragic even – ofttimes become the butt of jokes. You have but to think of graveyard humor, the jests concerning death and the deceased. And the heavenly bodies themselves have not been spared this treatment. Take for example the Sun, or the Moon. The Moon is now and then depicted as a skinny character with a drooping fool's cap and a chin that sticks out like a sickle, while the Sun is a fat-faced, friendly humpty-dumpty in a tousled aureola. And yet, though the kingdoms of both life and death serve as objects of ridicule, and things both great and small, there is something at which no one yet has had the courage to laugh or jeer. Nor is this thing the sort which one might easily forget or fail to notice, for I am speaking here of everything that exists, in other words the Universe. Yet if you think upon it, O King, you will see how very ludicrous is the Universe . . .'

At this point, for the first time, King Globares experienced surprise, and with growing interest listened to the words of the sage, who said:

'The Universe is composed of stars. That sounds serious enough, but when we look into the matter more closely, it is hard to keep from smiling. In actual fact – what are stars? Spheres of fire, suspended in the everlasting night. A compelling image, it would seem. Compelling by its nature? No, purely on account of its size. But size alone cannot decide the significance of a phenomenon. Do the scribblings of a cretin, transferred from a sheet of paper to a broad plain, become thereby momentous?

'Stupidity multiplied does not cease to be stupidity, only its ludicrousness is increased. And the Universe, what is it but a scribble of random dots! Wherever you look, however far you go – this and nothing else! The monotony of Creation would seem to be the most crass and uninspired idea one could possibly imagine. A dotted nothingness going on and on into infinity – who would contrive such a witless thing if it had yet to be created? Only a cretin, surely. To take, if you please, the immeasurable stretches of emptiness and dot them, over and over, haphazardly here and there – how can one attribute order to such a structure, or grandeur? It fills one with awe? Say rather with despair, in that there is no appealing it. Indeed it is only the result of self-plagiarism, a self-plagiarism done from a beginning that was in turn the most mindless of acts possible, for what can you do with a blank sheet of paper before you and pen in hand when you do not know, when you haven't the faintest idea where to begin? A drawing? Bah, you must first know what there is to draw. And if you have nothing whatever in mind? If you find yourself without a grain of imagination? Well, the pen, placed upon the page as though of its own accord, unintentionally touching, will make a dot. And that dot, once made, will create – in the mindless musing that accompanies such creative impotence – a pattern, suggestive by virtue of the fact that besides itself there is absolutely nothing, and that with the littlest effort it can be repeated ad infinitum. Repeated, yes, but how? Dots, after all, may be arranged in some design. But what if this too is beyond you? Nothing remains but to shake the pen in frustration, spattering ink, filling up the page with dots blindly, any which way.'

With these words the sage took a large piece of paper

and, dipping his pen in an inkwell, spattered ink upon it several times, after which he pulled out of his robe a map of the firmament and showed the first and the second to the King. The resemblance was striking. Millions of dots appeared across the paper, some larger, some smaller, for at times the pen had spattered copiously and at times had gone dry. And the sky on the map was represented exactly the same way. From his throne the King regarded both sheets of paper and was silent. The sage meanwhile went on:

'You have been taught, O King, that the Universe is a structure infinitely sublime, mighty in the majesty of its star-woven vasts. But observe, is not that venerable, all-pervading and eternal frame the work of the utmost stupidity, does it not in fact constitute the very antithesis of thought and order? Why has no one noticed this before? – you ask. Because the stupidity is everywhere! But its omnipresence all the more stridently cries out for our ridicule, our distancing laughter, a laughter which would at the same time usher in revolt and liberation. How very fitting it would be to write, in just this spirit, a Lampoon of the Universe, in order that that work of supreme inanity receive the rebuff it deserves, in order that from then on it be attended not with a chorus of worshipful sighs, but with hoots and catcalls.'

The King listened, dumbfounded, and the sage – after a moment of silence – continued:

'The duty of every scientist would be the writing of such a Lampoon, were it not for the fact that then he would have to put his finger on the first cause, which brought into being this state of things that merits only derision and regret, called the Universe. And that took place when Space was still completely empty and awaiting the first creative acts, while the world, sending forth buds from less than nothingness through nothingness, had produced barely a handful of clustered bodies, on which reigned your great-great-great-ancestor, Allegoric. He then conceived a thing impossible and mad, for he decided to replace Nature in its infinitely slow and patient work! He decided, in Nature's stead, to create a Cosmos abundant and full of priceless wonders. Unable to accomplish this himself, he ordered built a machine of the greatest intelligence, that it might carry out the task. Three hundred years were spent in the construction of that Moloch, and three hundred more, the reckoning of time however was different then. Nothing was spared, neither in effort nor in resources, and the mechanical monster reached proportions and power all but boundless. When the machine was ready, the usurper of Nature gave the order to turn it on. He had no inkling of what exactly it would do. It was, as a result of his limitless arrogance, by now too large, and consequently its wisdom, towering far above the greatest minds, exceeding the culmination, the pinnacle of genius, tumbled down into a total disintegration of intellect, into a jabbering darkness of centrifugal currents, that tore apart all content, so that the monstrosity, coiled up like some metagalaxy and laboring in frenzied circles, gave up the ghost at the first unuttered words – and from that chaos, seemingly thinking with the most terrible exertion, in which swarms of still unfinished concepts all turned back into oblivion, from those struggling, straining, useless convulsions and collisions there began to trickle down to the obedient print-out subsystems of the colossus only senseless punctuation marks! This was not, now, the most intelligent of intelligent machines possible, the Cosmocreator Omnipotens, but a ruin begotten of a heedless usurpation, a ruin which, destined for great things, could only stammer dots. What happened then? The ruler eagerly awaited some all-fulfilling execution of his plans, the boldest plans that ever thinking being devised, and no one dared to tell him he was standing at the source of a meaningless yammer, a mechanical agony that entered the world in its very death throes. But the lifelessly obedient hulks of the print-out machines were ready to carry out any command, and so, in time to the transmitted beat they began from the material clay to manufacture that which in three-dimensional space corresponds to the two-dimensional image of a point: spheres. And in this way, repeating endlessly one thing and always the same, till heat appeared and set each mass ablaze, they hurled into the chasms of the void round after round of fiery spheres, and thus in a stutter did the Universe arise! Your great-great-great-grandfather was, then, the creator of the Universe, yet at the same time the author of an absurdity whose magnitude nothing now will ever equal. For the act of destroying so aborted a piece of work would certainly be much more sensible and – the main thing – desired and consciously intended, which indeed you cannot say about that other act, Creation. And this is all I have to tell you, O King, descendant of Allegoric, the builder of worlds.'

When the King had sent away the sages, showering them first with gifts, and the oldest especially, who had in one stroke succeeded in rendering him the highest compliment and the greatest insult, one of the young scholars asked that sage, when at last they were alone, how much truth there was to his tale.

'What am I to tell you?' answered the old one. 'That which I said, did not come from knowledge. Science does not concern itself with those properties of existence to which ridiculousness belongs. Science explains the world, but only Art can reconcile us to it. What do we really know about the origin of the Universe? A blank so wide can be filled with myths and legends. I wished, in my mythologizing, to reach the limits of improbability, and I believe that I came close. You know this already, therefore what you really wanted to ask was if the Universe is indeed ludicrous. But that question each must answer for himself.'

The Tale of King Gnuff

After the good king Helixander's death, his son, Gnuff, ascended the throne. Everyone was unhappy about this, because Gnuff was ambitious and cowardly. He decided he would earn for himself the epithet of Great, yet he was afraid of drafts, of ghosts, of wax, for on a waxed floor one could break one's leg, of relatives, in that they might interfere in his governing, and most of all – of having his fortune told. Immediately as he was crowned, he ordered that throughout the kingdom doors be shut and windows not opened, that all the fortunetelling consoles be destroyed, and to the inventor of a machine that got rid of ghosts he gave a medal and a pension. The machine was truly good, for not once did Gnuff see a ghost. Also he never went out into the garden, for fear of catching cold, and took walks only in the castle, which was very large. Once, while strolling through the corridors and suites of rooms, he wandered into the old part of the palace, which he had never visited before. In the first hall that he discovered stood the household guards of his great-great-grandfather, all wind-up, dating from the days before electricity. In the second hall he saw steamknights, also rusted, but this was not of interest to him, and he was about to turn and leave when he noticed a small door with the inscription: DO NOT ENTER. It was covered with a thick layer of dust and he would not have bothered with it, but for that sign. The sign outraged him. What was this – someone dared forbid *him*, the King? He opened the creaking door not without difficulty, and a winding stairway led him to an abandoned tower. And there stood a very old copper cabinet; it had little ruby eyes, a wind-up key and a tiny hatch. He realized this was a fortunetelling cabinet and again was angered, that despite his order it had been left in the palace, but then he thought, why not at least try it once and see what the cabinet does? So he went up to it on tiptoe, turned the key, and when nothing happened, banged on the hatch. The cabinet gave a husky sigh, the mechanism started grinding, and it looked at the King with a ruby eye, as if askance. That sidewise glance reminded him of Uncle Cenander, his father's brother, who formerly had been his tutor. He thought, it must be Uncle who had the cabinet put here, to spite me, for why else would it give that look? A funny feeling came over him, and the cabinet, stuttering, very slowly began to play a dismal tune, as if someone were striking an iron

tombstone with a shovel, and out through the hatch fell
a black card with bone-yellow rows of writing on it.

The King took fright in earnest, but could not now
overcome his curiosity. He grabbed up the card and ran
to his chambers. When at last he was alone, he took it
from his pocket. 'I'll look, but just to be safe, only with
one eye,' he decided, and looked. On the card was
written:

> *Now strikes the hour, now strike the kin,*
> *A family war is ushered in.*
> *Aunts and uncles, nephews, nieces*
> *Hack each other into pieces;*
> *Cousin does in second cousin,*
> *Digs a grave, then digs a dozen;*
> *In-laws fall and offspring drop,*
> *Stepsons will at nothing stop;*
> *There, daughters quartered with a laugh,*
> *Here, a half brother cut in half;*
> *The ax for gramps, the ax for granny,*
> *The ax for sister and her nanny;*
> *Brother murders brother, mother,*
> *One good turn deserves another.*
> *Relatives have certain worth,*
> *But they're more certain in the earth.*
> *The hour strikes, now sound the knell,*

Bury your relations well;
You yourself must hide and bide
Everywhere, yet stay inside,
The ties that bind go very deep,
Beware of treason in your sleep.

So badly was King Gnuff frightened, that everything grew dark before his eyes. He repented of the lack of caution that had led him to wind up the fortunetelling cabinet. It was, however, too late now, and he saw that he must act if the worst was to be avoided. Not for a moment did he doubt the import of the prophecy: he had long suspected that his closest relatives were a threat to him.

To tell the truth, it is not known whether all of this took place exactly as we have related here. But in any case sorry things – even grisly – happened after that. The King had his entire family put to death; only his one uncle, Cenander, managed to escape at the last minute, disguising himself as an upright piano. This failed to save him, he was shortly apprehended and surrendered his head to the block. On this occasion Gnuff was able to sign the sentence with a clear conscience, for his uncle had been seized while attempting to start a conspiracy against the Monarch.

Orphaned with such suddenness, the King went into

mourning. He was now much easier in his mind, though saddened too, for at heart he was neither wicked nor cruel. The King's peaceful mourning did not last long, it occurring to Gnuff that he might have relatives about whom he knew nothing. Any one of his subjects could be some distant cousin several times removed. So for a while he beheaded this one and that, but the beheadings did not set his mind at rest, for one could hardly be a king without subjects, and how could he kill them all? He became so suspicious that he ordered himself riveted to the throne, so no one could topple him from it; he slept in an armored nightshirt, and thought continually of what to do. Finally he did something extraordinary, so very extraordinary that he probably did not hit upon the idea himself. They say it was whispered to him by a traveling peddler dressed as a sage, or perhaps a sage dressed as a peddler – there are different accounts. The castle servants reportedly saw a masked figure, whom the King admitted to his chambers at night. The fact is that one day Gnuff summoned all the court architects, all the master electrologists, platesmiths and tuners, and announced that they were to enlarge his person, and enlarge it to extend beyond all horizons. The commands were carried out with amazing speed, as the King appointed to the post of director of the Planning Commission his trusty executioner. Processions of electricians and builders began carrying wires and spools into the castle, and when the built-up King had filled the entire palace with his person, so that he was, at one and the same time, in the vestibule, the cellar and the wings, they turned next to the residences close at hand. In two years Gnuff covered the downtown area. Houses not stately enough, and therefore unworthy to be occupied by the monarch's mind, were leveled to the ground; in their place were erected electronic palaces, called Gnuff's Amplifiers. The King spread little by little but inexorably, many-storied, precisely connected, enhanced with identity substations, till he became the whole capital city, and did not stop at its borders. His mood improved. He had no relatives, and now no wax or drafts to fear, for he didn't need to take a step anywhere, being everywhere at once. 'I am the state', he said, and not without reason, for besides himself, a self that inhabited the squares and avenues with rows of electrical edifices, no one any longer lived in the capital; except of course the royal dusters, sweepers and household wipers-off of grime; these tended the King's cogitation, which flowed from building to building. Thus there circulated throughout the city, for miles and miles, the satisfaction of King Gnuff, for he had succeeded in achieving greatness temporal and literal, and in addition was hidden everywhere, as the prophecy required, for indeed he was all-present in the kingdom. And what a pretty picture it made at dusk, when the King-titan through a soft glow winked its bulbs in thought, then slowly dimmed, sinking into a well-earned sleep. But that darkness of oblivion, after the first few hours of night, gave way to a fitful flickering, now here, now there, erratic flashes blinking on and off. These were the monarch's dreams beginning their swarm. Turbulent streams of apparitions coursed through the buildings, till in the murk the windows lit up and whole streets exchanged alternate bursts of red and violet light, while the household sweepers, plodding their way along the empty sidewalks, sniffed the burnt smell of the heated cables of His Royal Majesty and, sneaking a look inside the light-flooded windows, said to one another in low voices:

'Oho! Some nightmare must have Gnuff in its clutches – if only he doesn't take it out on us!'

One night, after a particularly hard-working day – for the King had been thinking up new kinds of medals with which to decorate himself – he dreamed that his uncle, Cenander, had sneaked into the capital, taking advantage of the darkness, wrapped in a black cloak, and was roaming the streets in search of supporters, to organize a vile conspiracy. Out of the cellars crawled a host of masked ones, and there were so many of them and they showed such readiness for regicide, that Gnuff started trembling

and awoke in terror. It was already dawn and the golden
sun played upon the little white clouds in the sky, so he
said to himself: 'A dream, nothing more!' – and resumed
his work of designing medals, and those he had invented
the previous day were pinned onto his terraces and bal-
conies. When however after his daylong toil he again
settled down for the night, no sooner did he doze off
than he saw the conspiracy in full flower. It had happened this way: when Gnuff, before, wakened from the
conspiring dream, he did so incompletely; the downtown sector, in which had hatched that antigovernment
dream, did not wake up at all, but continued to lie in its
nightmare grip, and only the King awake knew nothing
of this. Meanwhile a considerable part of his person,
namely the old center of the city, quite unaware that the
uncle-malefactor and his machinations were only a
phantom, remained under the delusion of the nightmare. That second night Gnuff dreamed he saw his
uncle in a state of feverish activity, mustering the relatives. And they all appeared, every last one, posthumously
creaking their hinges, and even those with the most
important parts missing raised up their swords against
the rightful ruler! There was great commotion. Hordes
of masked ruffians rehearsed in whispers rebel cheers;
down in the vaults and cellars they were already sewing
the black banners of insurrection; everywhere poisons

were being brewed, axes sharpened, grenades assembled, and preparations made for an all-out encounter with the hated Gnuff. The King took fright a second time, awoke shaking, and was about to call – using the Golden Archway of the Royal Mouth – all his troops to his aid, to have them cut the conspirators to ribbons with their swords, but he quickly saw that this would serve no purpose. The soldiers, after all, could not enter his dream, could not crush the conspiracy growing there. So for a time he tried by sheer force of will to rouse those four square miles of his being that persisted in dreaming of rebellion – but in vain. Though truly he had no way of knowing whether it was in vain or not, for while awake he could not detect the conspiracy; it appeared only when sleep overtook him.

While conscious, he could not gain entry to the insurgent sectors, which is not surprising, since reality cannot penetrate its way into a dream's interior, only another dream can do that. The King realized that in this situation the best thing was for him to fall asleep and dream a counterdream, and not just any kind, obviously, but one monarchistic, wholly devoted to him, flags waving in the wind; with a royal dream like that, rallied around the throne, he would then be able to wipe out the treasonous nightmare.

Gnuff set to work, but his fear kept him awake; so he

began in his mind to count pebbles, till this exhausted him and he fell into a deep slumber. It turned out then that the dream under the leadership of his uncle had not only entrenched itself in the downtown district, but was even beginning to imagine arsenals filled with powerful bombs and demolishing mines. Whereas he himself, try as he might, succeeded in dreaming up no more than a single company of cavalry, and unmounted at that, poorly disciplined, and armed only with pot lids. 'This isn't working,' he thought, 'I'll have to start again from scratch!' So he set about waking, which was slow and difficult, at last he awoke all the way, but then a terrible suspicion came upon him. Had he in fact returned to reality, or was this instead a different dream, the semblance only of wakefulness? How to proceed in such a tangled situation? To sleep or not to sleep? That was the question! Suppose he did not now sleep, feeling himself to be secure, for indeed in the world of reality no conspiracy existed. No harm would be done: that regicidal dream would dream itself out, dreaming on to its dreamed conclusion, until in the final awakening the sovereign state regained its proper unity. Very good. Ah, but if he did not dream a counterdream, going on the assumption that he was safely awake, while in actual fact his alleged awakedness was but a different dream, adjoining the other, the uncle dream, then this could lead to catastrophe! For at any moment the whole accursed band of regicides, with that odious Cenander at its head, could tear from that dream into this, the dream that feigned reality, in order to deprive him of his throne and life!

'It is true,' he reflected, 'the depriving would take place only in a dream, yet if the conspiracy overruns my entire royal psyche, if it takes control from the mountains to the oceans, and if – O dreadful thought! – my self no longer wishes to awake, what then?! In that case I will be cut off from reality forever and Uncle will do with me what he wishes. He'll torture me, humiliate me. To say nothing of my aunts – I remember them well: no mercy shown, never, no matter what. That's how they are – or rather, were – no, are again in this horrible dream! And anyway, why speak of dreams? A dream can only be where there is also a reality to return to (and how shall I return, if they succeed in keeping me in the dream?); where there is nothing but dream, dream is the sole reality, and therefore it is not a dream. Hideous! All this, of course, comes of that wretched excess of personality, that expansionism of the mind – much good it has done me!'

In despair he saw that inaction could very well destroy him, and that his only hope lay in the immediate mobilization of his psyche. 'I must proceed as though I were asleep,' he said to himself. 'I must dream a multitude of devoted subjects, all full of love and enthusiasm, battalions loyal to the bitter end, dying with my name upon their lips, and plenty of armaments. It might even be a good idea to think up quickly some miracle weapon, for in a dream surely everything is possible: let's have a substance for removing relatives, anti-uncle cannons, something of that sort. In this way I'll be prepared for whatever happens, and if the conspiracy shows itself, insidiously creeping from dream to dream, I'll smash it in a single blow!'

King Gnuff heaved a sigh with every square and boulevard of his being, so complicated was all this, and got down to work – that is, he went to sleep. In his dream, troops of steel were to stand in formation, with hoary generals at their head, and crowds cheering to the thunder of trumpets and kettledrums. But all that appeared was a tiny bolt. Nothing – only this bolt, perfectly ordinary, a little jagged around the edges. What was he to do with it? He thought and thought, meanwhile he felt a strange uneasiness, a growing uneasiness, a faintness, a mounting fear, till suddenly it dawned on him: 'Bolt rhymes with revolt!!'

He quaked all over. So then, the symbol of his downfall his overthrow, his death! Therefore the mob of relatives was even now coming for him, in stealth, in silence, having tunneled through that other dream to reach this dream – and any minute he would plunge into the treacherous pit, dug out of dream from under dream! Then the end was imminent! Death! Annihilation! But from where? How? In which direction?!

Ten thousand buildings of his royal person blazed; the substations, decked with medals and festooned with ribbons of the Cross of Greatness, shook; the decorations rang out rhythmically in the night air, such was King Gnuff's struggle with the dreamed dread symbol of his downfall. At last he overcame it, mastered it, till it vanished so completely, it was almost as if it had never been. The King looked – where was he now? In reality or in another illusion? In reality, it would seem, yes but how could he be certain? It was possible, of course, that the uncle dream by now had finished dreaming, that there was absolutely no need to worry. But again: how could he find out? There was one way and one way only, with dream-spies disguised as subversives to comb and ceaselessly probe his entire, own, sovereign self, the kingdom of his being, and nevermore would the royal soul know peace, he would always have to be on guard against conspiracy slumbering in some secret corner of his vast consciousness! And so onward, come, buoy up the figments of fealty and devotion, dream of homages rendered and thronging delegations aglow with law-abiding

49

zeal, attack with dreams all the valleys, darknesses and reaches of your person, that in them no intrigue, no uncle be allowed to hide! And then swept over Gnuff the rustle of standards so dear to his heart, no trace of Uncle, not a relative in sight, he was surrounded only by loyalty, he received oblations, ovations, tributes never-ending; one could hear the peal of beaten gold medallions rolling at his feet, sparks flew from chisels as artists hewed him monuments. The King's soul brightened within him, for here now was heraldry, embroidered-emblazoned, a tapestry hung in every window, artillery lined up to fire its salute, and trumpeters putting to their lips their trumpets of bronze. When however he took a closer look at all of this, he saw that something – somehow – wasn't right. The monuments – not bad, but not much like him either; in the twist of the face, in the scowl there was something decidedly avuncular. The standards blowing – all right, but that tiny ribbon with them, indistinct, almost black; if not black, at least dirty, in any case – not clean. What was this? Some sort of innuendo?!

Good heavens! But those tapestries – worn through in places, practically bald, and Uncle – Uncle had been bald . . . No, this could not be! 'Back! Retreat! Wake up! Wake up!!' he thought. 'Sound the alarm, reveille, away with this dream!' he wanted to shout, but when everything had vanished, it was no better. He had fallen out of one dream into another, a new dream, a dream dreamed by the dream preceding, which in turn had occurred in an earlier dream, therefore this present dream was already – as it were – to the third power. Everything in it changed, openly now, into treason, everything reeked of betrayal, the standards turned inside out – like gloves – from royal to black, the medals came with threaded screws, like severed necks, and from the golden bugles burst not battle charges, but his uncle's laughter, a thunderclap-guffaw that spelled disaster. The King roared in a voice stentorian, he called for his soldiers – let them prick him with their lances, so he could wake! 'Pinch me! Pinch me!!' he demanded with a mighty howl, and: 'Reality!! Reality!!!' – but to no avail; so once again he strained and struggled from the traitorous, king-hating, assassinating dream to the dream of the throne, but by now the dreams in him had multiplied like rats, scurrying-scuttling everywhere, by now building infected building with the nightmare, in all directions spread a sneaking, a skulking, a slinking around, some sort of skulduggery, just what it was he didn't know, but God-awful for sure! The electronic edifice in all its hundred stories dreamed of bolts, revolts, insurrection and defection, in every identity substation there schemed a band of relatives, in every amplifier an uncle cackled; the foundations trembled, terrified of themselves, and out of them a hundred thousand kin came swarming, false pretenders to the throne, two-faced first-born foundlings, glowering usurpers, and though not one of them knew whether he was a creature dreamed or dreaming, and who was dreaming whom, and why, and what all that implied – they all without exception made straight for Gnuff, to cut him down, to pull him from the throne, hang him, swing him from the highest belfry, ding to kill him, dong to bring him back again, hey! fill him with lead, ah! off with his head – and the only reason they had done nothing yet was that they couldn't agree on where to start. Thus in torrents rushed the phantom monsters of the royal mind, until from the overload there was a burst of flame. No longer a dreamed but a very real fire now filled the windows of the King's person with a golden blaze, and Gnuff collapsed into a hundred thousand separate dreams, linked by nothing now but a conflagration – and he burned for a long, for a very long time . . .